# MARVEL
# GUARDIANS OF THE GALAXY

## THE JUNIOR NOVEL

ADAPTED BY CHRIS WYATT

WRITTEN BY JAMES GUNN AND NICOLE PERLMAN

BASED ON THE MARVEL COMIC
BY DAN ABNETT AND ANDY LANNING

Ⓛ Ⓑ
**LITTLE, BROWN AND COMPANY**
New York . Boston

marvelkids.com

© 2014 MARVEL

Little, Brown and Company

Hachette Book Group
237 Park Avenue, New York, NY 10017
Visit our website at lb-kids.com

Little, Brown and Company is a division of Hachette Book Group, Inc.
The Little, Brown name and logo are trademarks of Hachette Book Group, Inc.

The publisher is not responsible for websites (or their content)
that are not owned by the publisher.

First Edition: July 2014

Library of Congress Control Number: 2014937167

ISBN: 978-0-316-29324-2

10 9 8 7 6 5 4 3 2 1

RRD-C

Printed in the United States of America

# PROLOGUE

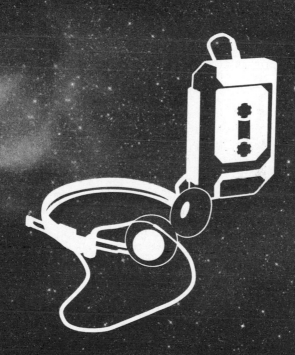

It was very cold on Peter Quill's last day on planet Earth. It was so cold that the nine-year-old could almost see his breath indoors.

Sitting on a hard plastic bench listening to his Awesome Mix Tape #1, Peter saw into the hospital room where family members buzzed around Momma's bed. She had been sick for a long time—sometimes she'd call her son by the wrong name—but now things were so much worse.

"Peter, your mom wants to talk to you."

Peter looked over to see Gramps. How long had he been standing there?

"Get these fool things off," Gramps said, removing Peter's headphones. His voice was firm, but warm.

"Come on, son. She needs to see you. But be patient with her. She's even more confused than usual."

Gramps shuffled Peter into the room, where his normally beautiful mother looked pale and weak. She stared at him with sunken eyes that didn't seem to focus. She smiled and brushed back his hair with her fingertips, brushing a bruise near his eye.

She frowned at the welt, and asked, "Have you been fighting with the other boys again?"

Peter shrugged.

"Peter?" she asked, sternly looking at him for a reply.

"They hurt a little frog that ain't done nothing." Peter explained about the bullies in his neighborhood. "They smushed it with a stick."

"You're just like your father," Momma whispered. Her eyes drifted up toward the skies, a dreamy expression crossing her face. "He was an angel of light."

Peter saw Gramps exchange a quick look with Momma's doctor, a look that said, *She's getting "confused" again.* Gramps reached out and touched Momma, shaking her shoulder a little, like he was trying to wake her up.

"Meredith, have you got a present there for Peter?" asked Gramps.

Momma looked down into her lap as if seeing the present that sat there for the first time. But then she seemed to recognize it and handed it to her son. Peter took it in his hands and looked at the sloppy packaging and crooked bow.

"Sorry I didn't wrap it better," she apologized. "My hands have been like mittens." She held up her hands, showing him, as if he could actually see mittens there. But he couldn't—he just saw the hands that had hugged him so many times, and soon never would again.

Peter held the present, not entirely sure what to do with it.

"I got you covered, Pete," Gramps said as he picked up the present and stuck it in Peter's open backpack.

Momma nodded at the present. "That's for you to open after"—she choked up for a moment—"after I'm gone, okay? Your granddad's gonna take good care of you, at least until your daddy comes back to get you."

She swallowed deeply and then held out her hand to Peter. "Take my hand, baby."

Peter looked again at his momma's hands, but he froze. He couldn't move.

"Take my hand, baby," Momma said once again.

A tear rolled down Peter's cheek. He wanted to take his mother's hand. He really did. But somehow he just couldn't. All he could do was stand there, letting the hot tears fill his eyes.

"Peter, take my—" his mother started again, but then, abruptly, the beeping of her monitors halted, and she fell back against the bed.

The doctor and some nurses rushed for the bed, pushing Peter back away from his mother.

Quickly, Gramps covered Peter's eyes and pulled him into the hallway. "You've got to harden yourself, Pete," said Gramps. "Stay here," he added as he ran back into the room. From outside, Peter could hear the rest of his family begin to weep.

That's when Peter ran.

He didn't think about running. He just did. No one stopped him.

He ran out of the hospital and across the parking lot.

He ran up the far embankment and out past the weeds and grass.

He ran through a stand of pines and out into a field.

And when he finally ran out of breath, Peter dropped to his knees and broke into a deep sob.

Peter was still crying when a giant spotlight from the sky shone down on him.

He looked up to see a large spaceship, bigger than a tanker truck, hovering above him. The ship flashed bright lights and crackled with electricity. It hung in the air as if watching the boy, and then started to lower slowly until Peter vanished into the light.

# CHAPTER 1

The planet Morag was once home to a great civilization. For centuries, the citizens worked together to develop commerce, build monuments, and advance the arts. But at the height of its culture, Morag's environment went through a terrible shift.

Suddenly, violent storms of unimaginable power blasted the globe. Mega earthquakes struck, sea levels rose, and continents flooded. The mass destruction led to a planetary evacuation. Over the centuries, Morag fell to ruins and was visited only by adventurous water-breathing archeologists and horribly unlucky spaceship-wreck survivors.

But when Morag's lesser sea began to recede, a different kind of visitor came.

His ship landed on the rain-soaked, windswept outskirts of a city, and anchored itself into the stone. The pilot descended his ship's ramp, his face covered in a protective mask, and walked through the torrent of rain into the ruins of Morag Prime. Once he reached the location of its main thoroughfare, he pulled out his holo-mapping device.

The gadget shot out tracking dots that scanned its surroundings and projected a grainy hologram of the way the streets of Morag Prime had looked in their heyday. Then: "BA-BEEP!" The holo-map calculated a way through the ruins, marking the route with a red holo-line.

The visitor looked around, popped on a pair of headphones, and began listening to his favorite songs on Awesome Mix Tape #1 for what seemed like the millionth time. As he pulled off his mask, Peter Quill smiled.

In the twenty-something years since he was abducted from Earth, he'd seen a lot. He'd seen a planet made of fire with a moon made of ice. He'd seen an army of shape-shifting aliens attack a space whale. He'd even watched as twin suns went supernova together. It had been a pretty amazing couple of decades.

He'd worked his way through the ranks on the Ravager outlaw ship that had picked him up. He had started as the space equivalent of a deck hand and risen all the way to being his captain's second in command.

But in all these years, there was one thing he'd never been. He'd never been rich. And, as he walked into the remnants of a massive temple, he was ready to give it a try.

The chamber was dark inside, but Peter took out a plasma light sphere and shook it, igniting a brightness that illuminated the whole room.

"There it is," he mumbled as he looked up at the high ceiling to see a silver metallic Orb hovering far above his head. The Orb floated inside a protective laser fence that still functioned after all these hundreds of years.

This was it. This is what he'd come for. He'd give it to the Broker, and the Broker would make him rich.

What was the Orb for? What was in it? What did it do? Peter didn't know, and he didn't care. When he looked at that Orb, all he saw was his future.

"Let's get you down here, big boy," Peter said, pulling a tool out of his pack.

As soon as he turned on his electromagnet, the silver Orb shuttered and moved toward it. For a moment the Orb strained at the edge of the laser fence, but then it popped out and dropped to the ground, sticking to the magnet.

"Ha-ha!" Peter shouted happily as he turned off the gadget and picked up the Orb. He was so happy to have his hands on the artifact that he wanted to kiss it, and he might have done just that... except that he'd noticed he was not alone.

"Drop it!" said the dangerous commander Korath as his Sakaaran soldiers leveled their weapons.

"Cool, no problem!" Peter said. He let the Orb go and put his hands in the air.

"Who are you?" Korath demanded.

Peter tried to act casual, like he didn't understand how valuable the Orb might be. "Hey, I'm just exploring, man!"

"How did you know about this?" asked Korath, pointing to the Orb.

"I don't even know what that is! I'm just a junker," explained Peter. "I search for salvage, anything that can be recovered and resold."

Korath took a moment to look Peter over from top to bottom.

"We don't believe you," Korath grunted. "You're wearing Ravager gear."

The Ravagers were a gang of criminals that pulled off jobs in this sector, and if you crossed them, you usually weren't heard from again. Peter was, in fact, a Ravager . . . but he didn't want Korath to know that.

Korath spoke to his soldiers in the Sakaaran language. The soldiers moved forward, grabbing Peter by the arms.

"We're taking you back to our ship," Korath said.

"What?" shouted Peter. This was not going well. "Why?"

"My master, Ronan, might have some questions for you."

"Oh, hey..." said Peter. "There is another name you might know me by..."

"What is that?"

Peter looked him right in the eyes and prepared to enjoy the impact his revelation would make.

"I am..." The aliens leaned in closer, waiting. *"Star-Lord!"*

Korath looked confused. "Who?"

Not the impact Peter was looking for.

"Star-Lord! Come on, man...*the* Star-Lord! The legendary outlaw!"

Korath turned back to his soldiers. "Any idea what he's talking about?"

The soldiers just shook their heads.

"Oh, man! Just forget it!" Peter was disappointed.... What did a guy have to do to get a little notoriety around the galaxy? At least the aliens had dropped their guard for a moment. Peter seized the opportunity and moved into action.

He kicked his Plasma Light Sphere into the soldiers and it burst, spraying them with hot plasma. As they screamed in surprise and pain, Peter grabbed the Orb and dashed away!

Quickly, Korath pulled out his rifle and fired. Peter ducked and the shot blew a hole in the temple wall!

"Thanks for the quick exit," Peter shouted as he hit the button that made his boots shoot out a quick rocket thrust, pushing him up and out the hole Korath had made.

Outside, Peter landed a fair distance from the temple. He looked back over his shoulder to see Korath looking out through the hole in the wall.

"He'll never catch up," thought Peter as he ran with the Orb.

"Get him!" screamed Korath. Peter turned to see five more Sakaaran soldiers now between him and his ship. They shouted and raised their rifles.

"You've got to be kidding me," Peter muttered. He was still running at the soldiers, racking his brain for how to get out of this situation, when he realized the soldiers' armor was metal.

"Worth a try," he said, reaching backward into his pack to pull out the electromagnet. He switched it on and threw it ahead of him.

Immediately, the five soldiers were jerked forward toward the magnet! They dropped their weapons as they stuck to the device.

*I can't believe that worked!* Peter thought to himself. He jumped over the pile of soldiers as they struggled to pull themselves back up.

Finally past them, Peter ran up the loading dock

into his ship, the *Milano*. Once in the cockpit, he immediately fired up the engines and took off.

But he wasn't in the clear just yet. Peter peered through the cockpit window and saw that the soldiers weren't out of options. One of them had managed to turn off the electromagnet, and now, under Korath's supervision, they were loading a massive rocket launcher.

A rocket roared straight toward the *Milano*, with Peter barely banking the ship in time to avoid it. He pushed the engines forward, escaping the ruins just as a second rocket blasted past him!

"Later, losers!" shouted Peter as thrusters engaged and he escaped into the planet's atmosphere. Escaping from an army of Sakaaran soldiers with invaluable treasure—if that didn't add to the legend of "Star-Lord the Outlaw," nothing would!

Hours later, the ship set on course for the planet Xandar, where he would meet the Broker, Peter sat in his pilot chair idly tossing the Orb into the air and catching it over and over again. He was daydreaming of things to do with his coming fortune when a video call came in over the main console.

"Quill," grumbled Yondu, the blue-skinned alien who served as captain of the Ravagers.

"Hey, Yondu," Peter said casually.

"I'm here on Morag. The artifact I'm looking for ain't here, but I do see some of your handiwork: a couple of deep-fried Sakaaran soldiers."

"Yeah, I was in the neighborhood. Thought I'd save you the hassle," Peter said simply.

Yondu shifted his eyes. "Where are you?"

"You know, boss, I feel bad about this...but I'm not going to tell you that."

Yondu's face twisted in anger. "I slaved this putting together a deal with the Broker for the Orb!"

"'Slaved' is pushing it," chuckled Peter.

"And now you're going to rip me off?" Yondu demanded.

"Making a few calls is 'slaved'? I mean, come on—" continued Peter.

Yondu's blue face got redder and redder. "We don't do this to each other. We're Ravagers. We got a code!"

"Yeah, the code is: 'Steal from everybody,'" Peter reminded him.

"Everybody...not *me*!" Yondu yelled back.

"That's a particularly self-serving definition of 'everybody.'"

"When we picked you up from Earth, my boys wanted to eat you. I stopped them! You're alive because of me!"

"And now I'm rich because of you. You're the one who taught me that the universe belongs to the heartless," Peter pointed out.

"I'll put a bounty on you, boy! I'll find you!"

"Yeah, yeah. Later, Yondu," Peter said, cutting the call. Yondu's face disappeared from the screen.

Peter wasn't going to let anyone bring him down after the day he'd had. He went back to dreaming about what to do with all his money.

# CHAPTER 2

**H**anging in the blackness of space, the *Dark Aster* looked like a cross between a battle cruiser and a fortress. Wherever the warship appeared, it brought fear. Whole planets had been evacuated based only on rumors the *Dark Aster* was approaching.

It wasn't so feared because it was one of the most heavily armed warships ever created—which it was—but because it was the flagship of none other than Ronan. Some knew him as "Ronan the Murderer"; others as "Ronan the Butcher"; and still others as "Ronan the Warlord." All these names were meant to slur Ronan for his cruelty and heartlessness—but they pleased him, and there was one name he preferred above all the others: "Ronan the Accuser." Ronan looked upon the people of this galaxy and accused them of the greatest crime he could imagine—*weakness*.

Ronan was a member of a species of aliens that had once dominated huge sections of the galaxy. He was tall and incredibly strong and dwarfed those around him. He was the perfect specimen, strong in body and in mind.

Inside the warship, as Ronan rose from a giant pod full of oozing black fluid, one of his minions dragged in a prisoner. It was a captive officer of the Nova Corps, the law enforcement agency that policed the sector.

Ronan hated the Nova Corps because they stood in the way of his goal for total intergalactic conquest. And the Novas protected the weak, something that Ronan found disgusting.

The Nova officer, although clearly under Ronan's total power, looked up defiantly at the warlord looming over him.

"You're under arrest," croaked the battered officer bravely as he looked into Ronan's eyes, "for violations of sovereign space, unlawful seizure... and genocide."

Ronan smiled at the officer's nerve.

"You're in my court now," Ronan said to the officer. "I make the accusations here. The Nova Corps's pathetic protection of the weak at the expense of the strong has denigrated this galaxy and brought shame to any creature strong enough to call themselves a warrior."

Ronan brought his face close to the man. "Compassion is a disease," he finished.

"You will never rule the galaxy," shouted the officer, trying to cover his fear with boldness.

"Rule it? No," Ronan admitted as he raised his mallet-shaped Cosmi-Rod, a blunt weapon. "I will cure it!"

With a swing of his rod, Ronan silenced the officer.

As Ronan cleaned his weapon, another of his underlings entered.

"Korath has returned, my master," said the servant, "but he doesn't have the Orb."

Ronan frowned.

Ronan sat in the *Dark Aster*'s magnificent throne room and listened as Korath reported his failure to obtain the Orb from a petty thief.

"He is an outlaw," Korath explained. "He calls himself Star-Lord."

"Star-Lord?" Ronan asked, raising an eyebrow.

"Merely his own vain delusion," Korath said dismissively. "We have discovered he has an agreement to retrieve the Orb for an intermediary known as the Broker. I am unspeakably pleased to report that we will be able to intercept him at the Broker's shop on the planet Xandar."

Ronan looked down from his throne at Korath for what seemed like an eternity before asking, "You know the Orb is essential for our holy mission, yes, Korath?"

"Yes." Korath nodded humbly.

"And yet, you failed," stated Ronan.

"Yes, my lord, but..." Korath tried to explain.

"Take him to the ship's hold," Ronan commanded with a wave of the hand.

"No, master, please! No! Spare me!" Korath shouted as several of Ronan's soldiers removed him from their ruler's sight.

Ronan turned to look at his most trusted servants, Nebula and Gamora, two highly trained and ruthless warriors from different alien worlds.

"Korath's failure is unacceptable," said Ronan. "Until we have the Orb we cannot move in force against the Nova Corps."

He looked at the two women, as if making a decision. "Nebula, go to Xandar and dispense with this 'Star-Lord.' Get me that Orb," Ronan commanded.

"It will be my honor," said Nebula, bowing.

"It will be your doom," interrupted Gamora.

Nebula looked at Gamora with a rage-filled glance. "I am more than capable of this mission!"

"Korath was more than capable, but this thief outmatched him," Gamora said. "Why would it be any different for you?"

Ronan watched with interest as the women argued.

"And who would go instead of me? You?" Nebula asked.

"You are merciless and strong, Nebula," Gamora said. "But I've been to Xandar many times and know it well. If the field of engagement shifts, I'll be prepared."

Nebula retorted, "Ronan has already decreed that—"

"Don't speak for me," Ronan said, interrupting Nebula. He turned to look at Gamora, appraising her. "You will not fail?" he asked.

Gamora shrugged. "Have I ever?"

As Gamora loaded up her Necrocraft for the voyage to Xandar, Nebula shoved her into a nearby wall, pinning her.

"You think I don't know?" Nebula hissed into Gamora's face. "You think I don't realize that you would keep me from advancing? You would have Ronan tell our father, Thanos, that only Gamora furthers his great plan."

Thanos, an evil dictator, was the only person Ronan served. He had kidnapped both Nebula and Gamora when they were still babies and raised them to serve him as elite soldiers. As such, they were known around the galaxy as the "daughters" of Thanos.

Gamora shoved Nebula off her. "I would keep you alive, sister," Gamora replied.

Nebula sneered, "Compassion, Gamora? What would Ronan say to that?"

"You have known me since Thanos took us

both from our homes," began Gamora. "You have stood beside me in training, in modification, in battle...."

"I have stood *behind* you," shouted Nebula, her jealousy pouring out of her, "even though I am every inch the warrior you are. The screams of my enemies fill every field."

"Because you take so long to finish them," Gamora replied.

A wicked smile came to Nebula's lips. "It is not wrong to love your work."

"It is worse than wrong," Gamora said as she walked away, looking back over her shoulder. "It is weak."

Nebula stared angrily at Gamora as she walked away. Nebula fumed and began to make plans.

In the command chair on board the Necrocraft that would fly her to Xandar, Gamora entered orders into the computer console. The two Sakaaran troops that were to assist her on the mission approached.

"Course set for Xandar, my lady," reported one of the Sakaarans.

"And, might I add," he went on nervously, "it's an honor to be serving with Ronan's 'right hand' herself. My brother and I look forward to triumph," he finished, nodding to the other Sakaaran.

"Yes"—Gamora nodded—"but it's a shame about the casualties we're going to incur."

The Sakaarans looked at her with confusion. But before they could even ask a question, Gamora whipped her sword from her side and slashed them.

The Necrocraft slipped out of dock with Gamora as the only living passenger. Looking out the cockpit window, she contemplated the risks she was taking as she cleaned her blade. It would not be easy to betray Ronan.

# CHAPTER 3

It was a great day at the mall. The Xandarian sun was shining, the air was warm, and people were out having a good time. There were families playing, shoppers scoring deals, and friends dining outside at the mall's many fine restaurants—but there was someone who wasn't enjoying himself. Rocket, a four-foot-tall alien who looked like an Earth raccoon, was hiding in the bushes, peering at the crowds with binoculars.

"Humies, all of 'em, in a big hurry to get from something stupid to nothing at all. Pathetic," said Rocket, his upper lip curling in disgust. "Humies" was Rocket's insulting nickname for humanoid beings. If there was one thing that got on Rocket's nerves, it was humanoids.

Rocket moved his sights onto an average, non-descript male. "I mean, look at this guy! You believe they call us criminals when he's walking around assaulting me with that ugly face?" Rocket asked his partner, Groot.

But Groot, a seven-and-a-half-foot mobile tree creature, didn't seem to be paying much attention. He was focused on a nearby fountain.

"I mean, check out this moron," Rocket said as he adjusted his binoculars to look at a little boy playing on a seesaw. "This maniac's just wobbling around, annoying everyone in the world. Ha! Right, Groot?"

Rocket laughed, getting a kick out of himself, but when he turned to see if Groot was laughing, too, he saw his friend extending his roots into the fountain's water, slurping it up.

"Hey, don't drink that water! It's disgusting!" Rocket shouted.

Groot quickly pulled his roots out of the fountain and looked around innocently, as if he didn't understand what Rocket had said.

"Whatever. I saw you," said Rocket as his binoculars made a beeping sound. "Oh, looks like we got one," he observed.

The binoculars were set to scan for the faces of people who had outstanding bounties on their heads—people who were wanted by the law, or just by anyone with enough money to pay for their capture. Rocket peered through the binoculars to look at the face of yet another "humie," someone the facial recognition software identified as "Peter Quill, aka Star-Lord."

"Okay, let's see how much someone wants you," Rocket said as he checked the bounty on Peter Quill's head. "Forty thousand units! How can some miserable humie be worth that much? Hey, Groot, we're going to be rich!"

"I am Groot," said Groot.

**P**eter walked from the mall's main thoroughfare into the Broker's pawnshop.

"Hey, Broker," Peter said, greeting the humorless man behind the desk. "I've got your Orb, as commissioned."

Peter set the Orb down on the counter, but the Broker regarded him with suspicion. "Hello, Mr. Quill. Where is Yondu?"

"He wanted to be here, sends his love.... We good?"

The Broker looked from Peter to the Orb, then shrugged. "I guess we're good."

Not far from the pawnshop's door, Rocket handed Groot a sack large enough to hold a humie. "You just stuff him in here and run for the ship," Rocket instructed.

But when Rocket looked up, he saw that Groot wasn't listening. Instead, Groot was staring at a bug.

"Groot? What are you doing? Pay attention!"

Groot, by way of explanation, just pointed to the bug.

"Yeah, it's a bug. So what? This is forty thousand units on the line."

But Groot was still checking out the bug.

"You're not the idiot," mumbled Rocket. "I am, because I'm the one who partnered with a tree."

"I almost doubled the price when I saw what you guys were after. That's the best one of those I've ever seen," said Peter as the Broker examined the Orb to authenticate it. The Broker looked up at him, skepticism in his face.

"Okay...I don't know what it is," admitted Peter. "What is it?"

"It's my policy not to share info about my clients or their needs," said the Broker.

Peter grimaced. "Yeah, well, I almost got hurt for it."

The Broker shrugged. "I'm sure that's an occupational hazard in your line of work."

"Sometimes. But this was some freak working for some dude named Ronan," Peter continued.

The Broker straightened up instantly. "Ronan?"

"Yeah, you heard of him?"

"I'm sorry, Mr. Quill, I truly am, but I want no part of this if Ronan is involved," the Broker said as he shoved the Orb back into Peter's hands and pushed him out of the shop.

"Wait...why? I keep hearing the name, but who's Ronan?" asked Peter. But he was too late. He was already out in the mall with the Broker's door slammed in his face.

The Broker really seemed scared, Peter thought. He was considering his options when a green-skinned woman walked up to him.

"You have the bearing of a man of honor," Gamora said.

"Oh, I wouldn't say that," said Peter, shifting gears. "I hear it all the time, but I'd never say it."

Peter smiled as the woman got closer to him. This was someone he could get used to being near. But, with the blink of an eye, the woman grabbed the Orb, shoved Peter out of the way, and ran off!

"Hey, wait, lady! That's mine!" Peter screamed as he chased after her.

Gamora was fast, and she easily widened the gap between them.

"This is so not good," thought Peter as ran after his treasure. Thinking fast, he pulled some bolas out of his pack, whirled them around his head, and released them.

It was an expert throw. The bolas rushed through the air past several gawking shoppers and wrapped around Gamora's legs, bringing her to the ground. Peter was on her in a second. He reached for the Orb, but Gamora easily broke the bolas' ties around her legs and kicked him off.

Peter flew backward and reached into his pack for his pistol. But as he raised it, Gamora used her sword to slice it in two. She raised her arms, preparing to strike again, as Peter ducked.

"Oh no! She's going to hurt him! Don't let her hurt him!" shouted Rocket as he leaped into the scene. He tackled Gamora as Groot wrapped his branches protectively around Peter.

"Put him in the sack and run!" Rocket shouted to Groot.

Groot, confused, looked at the sack, then at Peter, and then at Gamora. Suddenly, he jumped to Gamora and tried to shove her head into the sack.

Peter didn't know who the raccoon and tree were, but whatever was happening, he had to get out. He grabbed the Orb and ran.

"Not *her—him!*" Rocket shouted at Groot. "Learn your pronouns, Groot!"

Groot stepped back, allowing Gamora to pick up Rocket and hurl him at Peter!

"Aughhh!" shouted Rocket as he slammed into the humanoid, knocking the Orb out of Peter's hands, over the balcony, and down to the lower level.

"No!" Peter screamed. As the Orb bounced away, Gamora vaulted over the railing after it.

"Oh, no you don't," said Peter as he jumped right onto her back.

Gamora slammed Peter into the ground. "You should have learned by now not to—"

"I don't learn," shouted Peter. "It's one of my issues!"

Peter shoved Gamora away and lunged for the Orb. With it back in his hands, he turned around and ran straight into Groot's bag. "Finally! Let's get out of here!" shouted Rocket.

With Peter inside their sack, the bounty hunters were prepared to leave. But Gamora stood in their path. "You gotta be kidding me, lady," yelled Rocket. "He's ours!"

Gamora side-kicked Rocket out of the way, then swung her sword at Groot, pruning off several branches. Groot shrieked as the splinters flew, and dropped Peter.

Gamora opened the sack quickly, ready to reclaim the Orb. But inside she found Peter looking up at her, a shock-stick in his hand.

Gamora froze as Peter aimed his weapon at her. He pulled himself from the sack and prepared to make his escape.

That's when he realized the whole group was surrounded.

Six Nova Corps Starblaster ships had them covered from all sides.

The loudspeaker of one of the Starblasters blared a message. "By order of the Nova Corps, you are all under arrest for endangerment to life and damage of property."

"Great, just great," said Rocket, paws above his head.

# CHAPTER 4

Floating in nothingness, Kyln station was a barbaric place. Battle-scarred, dirty, and heavily armored, it held some of the most hardcore criminals the galaxy had ever known.

"They call Kyln the stomach of the prison system," said Rocket, as he, Groot, Peter, and Gamora were shepherded by the Nova Corps through its halls, "because no matter how good you are going in, you come out pretty messed up."

The three of his companions shot him sour looks as if to say that fact wasn't much help in their situation.

"But I ain't gonna be here long," Rocket continued. "I've escaped twenty-two prisons. This one'll be no different." Rocket then focused his attention on Peter. "You're lucky Gamora here showed up, otherwise me and Groot'd be collecting that bounty right now, and you'd be getting drawn and quartered by Yondu and the Ravagers."

"A lot of people have tried to hurt me over the years, but I won't be brought down by a walking tree and a talking raccoon," said Peter, clearly annoyed.

"What's a raccoon?" asked Rocket, trying to decide if he should feel insulted.

"It's what you are," stated Peter.

"Ain't nothin' like me, 'cept me," huffed Rocket indignantly.

Peter turned to Gamora. "What is that Orb, anyway? Why is everyone so crazy for it?"

"I have no words for a thief without honor," said Gamora, not even bothering to look at Peter.

"Pretty high and mighty coming from you, maniac," Rocket responded. Gamora turned and glared at him, but he continued defiantly. "That's right, I know who you are. Ronan's little helper."

"Yeah, we all know who you are!" Peter confirmed, but then he turned and quietly whispered to Groot. "Who is she again?"

"I am Groot," Groot whispered back.

Peter rolled his eyes. "I know who *you* are. I'm asking who she is."

Rocket interrupted. "You won't get anything out of him. He don't know good talking like me and you. His vocabulistics are limited to 'I' and 'am' and 'Groot,' exclusively in that order."

"How do you understand him?"

Rocket shrugged. "I don't know. We just get each other."

"For your information, I wasn't getting the Orb for Ronan. I was going to sell it for myself," clarified Gamora.

But she didn't get to explain further, because at that very moment Peter saw one of the guards with his most prized possession—his head-phones! While private property was confiscated from all of the inmates, it was supposed to be impounded, not stolen by the guards.

"Hey, those are mine!" Peter shouted. But the guard just ignored him and wandered off, listening to Awesome Mix Tape #1.

Peter was *not* pleased.

The group was processed, given uniforms to wear, and escorted into the main yard. But as soon as they arrived, all the other inmates heckled them. Some even threw things. Peter bobbed to avoid a rock and a couple of boots.

At first Peter thought the prisoners were trying to hit *him*. Then he realized the target was actually Gamora. Everyone was aiming at her. Peter looked at Rocket in confusion.

"They don't like her kind," Rocket explained. "A lot of the prisoners have lost their cities and families to Ronan's forces. She'll last a day in here, at best."

"No.... The guards will protect her, right?" asked Peter.

Rocket laughed darkly at this. "They don't care what we do to each other."

Peter looked at Gamora, seeing that she had heard everything Rocket said. "It's okay," she told him, a sad look on her face. "Whatever nightmares my future holds shall be dreams compared to my past."

Sadly, everything Rocket said turned out to be true. That night, as Peter tried to fall asleep, he heard the sounds of a struggle in the hallway. When he went to the door, he witnessed a large, muscular, green-skinned prisoner with red battle tattoos dragging Gamora, kicking and fighting, down the corridor.

Instinctively, Peter decided to follow. "Quill?

Where you goin', Quill?" asked a bleary-eyed Rocket, awoken by Peter's stirring.

Rocket turned to find Groot asleep next to him. "Groot, Groot…wake up, Mr. Sleepy Tree…" Rocket said as he shook his friend. "Our bounty is up to something." But when Rocket couldn't wake the tree, he followed Peter by himself.

The tattooed man dragged Gamora to an isolated part of the station.

"Ronan murdered my family," growled the man, anger boiling behind his words. "On that day, every cell in my body united in the single purpose of one day destroying the man who was responsible. Because your master, Ronan, took them from me, I will now take you from him."

Gamora rushed to explain. "I, too, despise Ronan. And my so-called 'father,' Thanos. I have tried my whole life to escape from their grasp. The only reason I'm here is because I finally had an opportunity to be free."

"Your words mean nothing," said the man.

"Hey!" someone shouted from nearby.

Gamora and her captor turned to see Peter and Rocket watching them.

"Sorry, I didn't mean to interrupt," shouted Peter, "but I don't think you want to do that."

The man looked astonished.

"Do you know who I am?" the man asked Peter.

"No, but I know you're pretty scary-looking," Peter said. "Very intimidating."

"I am Drax the Destroyer, and no one in this prison gets in my way!"

"You heard the man," said Rocket, trying to pull Peter from the room.

But Peter shook Rocket off, and said, "I just mean that if getting Ronan really is your sole purpose, then I'm not sure this is the best way to go about it."

Drax looked confused. "Explain," he ordered.

"You don't want to hurt her because she betrayed Ronan," Peter explained. "And Ronan is a known lover of revenge. You keep her close, and you know what's going to happen?"

Drax looked at Peter, waiting.

"Ronan will come straight to you."

Drax realized Peter was right. Gamora was safe... for now.

As they were walked back to their quarters, Gamora spoke. "What you did...?" she started. "Well, you're not the man I assumed."

"Let's get one thing straight," Peter replied. "I don't care if you live or die. People who care about other people usually end up on the losing side of things."

Gamora was confused. "Then why stop Drax?"

"Because you're the only one who knows where to sell that stupid Orb."

Gamora nodded. Of course. This so-called "Star-Lord" really was just out for his own good.

"I know where to sell it," she said. "But since we're trapped here, what does it matter?"

Peter pointed to Rocket. "This one escaped twenty-two prisons."

"Yeah," confirmed Rocket, poking Peter in the gut. "We're escaping here, too—and headed straight to Yondu to get paid for your bounty."

"You said you had a buyer for the Orb," Peter said to Gamora. "How much was he going to pay you?"

"Four billion units," she replied.

"Four bill—*what*?!" exclaimed a shocked Rocket.

"Whoa! Seriously?" responded an equally shocked Peter.

"I trust that's worth more than his bounty?" Gamora asked Rocket.

Rocket just nodded, still in shock.

"Fine, then," Gamora continued. "Free all of us and I'll lead you to the buyer. We'll split the profits between the three of us."

But then a loud, protesting moan came from behind them. They turned to see Groot, angry. He'd found them and listened to every word.

"We split the money between the *four* of us," Rocket said, looking at Gamora.

Gamora nodded. "Agreed."

They all shared a long look. They may have met as competitors, but now they were in this together.

Star-Lord is a legendary interstellar adventurer.

He is really a human named Peter Quill from the planet Terra. Peter travels to Morag in search of a coveted Orb.

Peter plans to double-cross his old partner Yondu and sell the treasure for his own profit.

He does not know that Ronan the Accuser, one of the most dangerous beings in the galaxy, is also in search of this object.

While trying to sell the Orb, Peter gets in trouble with the Nova Corps, the group that serves and protects the galaxy, and is sent to the Kyln station.

There he meets several new friends. Rocket is a mechanical genius who also happens to look like a raccoon...

NAME
ROCKET
SUBJECT 89P13

GROOT

SEQUENCIN
M.DYN_//WE POS2

...and Groot is his tree-like best friend, who doesn't say much.

Drax is also a being of few words. His home world was destroyed, and he seeks revenge.

Gamora, the galaxy's deadliest woman, wants to fight for good.

Together, they must fight and protect the Orb from falling into Ronan's hands.

They are the Guardians of the Galaxy!

# CHAPTER 5

The next morning, over steel trays of some of the most disgusting "food" Peter had ever smelled, Rocket explained what he needed for his escape plan.

"To get out of here, we're going to need to get into the watchtower," the furry little alien said, jerking his head back at the central guard post. "And to get in there, I need three things: First, one of those," Rocket said, subtly pointing to an armband on one of the guards. The armbands acted as pass keys, letting the guards in and out of the secure areas.

"Second, I need that dude's fake leg," Rocket said, pointing to a prisoner who limped along using a robotic leg replacement.

"His leg?" asked Peter. "Are you serious?"

"Well, I certainly don't need the rest of him," said Rocket. "And last, do you see that black panel up there? The one with the flashing yellow lights?" asked Rocket, indicating a small area on the wall at least seventy feet off the ground. "Behind that panel is a quarnyx battery, a purplish box with a green wire around it. We need that."

Peter and Gamora looked at each other, displeased. "How do you expect us to get up there?" asked Peter. "Especially without being seen by everyone?"

"Hey, I got only one plan to get out of here, and I need a quarnyx battery for it!"

Rocket, Gamora, and Peter were so absorbed in a debate over how best to get the battery that they didn't even notice Groot leaving the table. He walked over to the wall and started to grow, quickly gaining enough height to reach the battery.

As Groot tore into the wall and ripped out what he needed, Rocket explained, "Once that battery is pulled out, the whole prison will lock down into emergency mode...so we need to get that last."

The battery came free with a *click*, and the lights in the entire station immediately went down. A split second after, red emergency lighting shone, an alarm went off, and armed guards started to swarm into the yard.

"What's going on?" Rocket looked up and was surprised to see Groot above them, waving the battery around and clearly very pleased with himself. "Or we get the battery first and then improvise," Rocket said with a sigh.

"Prisoner, put the device down," shouted a Nova Guard's voice from the speakers. Groot roared threateningly at the annoying hover-bots that swarmed him.

"Fire!" shouted the hover-bots as they unleashed a hail of lasers!

"I AM GROOT!!!" Groot screamed as he expanded his body, making shields of bark to protect him from the lasers.

Then chaos broke out. Prisoners attacked guards. It was as if, once the laser fire broke, everyone went crazy. They were in the middle of a full-scale riot!

"Well," said Gamora, looking at the fighting erupting all around them, "I'll get one of those armbands."

"I'll get the leg," shouted Peter as he ran off through the crowd.

The man looked at Peter suspiciously. "What do you want?" he asked.

"Uh...your leg," explained Peter. "Please," he added, hoping to sound respectful.

"Why would I do that?" asked the prisoner.

"Well, how does five thousand units in your family's bank account sound?" asked Peter.

"Not as good as a leg!" answered the prisoner.

Meanwhile, Gamora approached one of the guards in the fighting and knocked him sideways to the ground. "I need your armband," Gamora yelled.

"Yeah, good luck with that!" taunted the guard.

Gamora lifted the guard up by the arm. "Well, I'll think of something...." Gamora said, a threatening sound in her voice.

**P**eter was running down the corridor with the prisoner's leg, back out to where the others were, when he was spotted by a guard.

"Put down that—what is that, a leg? Put that down and move back into—"

But Peter didn't let him finish. He knocked the guard to the ground with the leg. "You'll pay for that," the guard's partner said.

"No, he won't," said Drax, stepping from behind the second guard.

Drax looked at Peter. "If your quest is liberation, you have a friend in me…and Ronan's servant is not leaving without me."

Peter and Drax ran together toward the watchtower.

Rocket raced up the still-giant Groot, almost like an Earth raccoon climbing an Earth tree. The mastermind stopped at Groot's shoulder. "The watchtower! Now!" Groot nodded and moved toward the tower, scooping up Gamora as he walked.

Once they reached their destination, Groot returned to his normal size as Rocket and Gamora used the armband to unlock the outer door.

At that moment, Peter, having just climbed the tower, pulled himself up over the railing.

"Here's the leg you needed," he said, throwing it to Rocket.

"Great!" said Rocket, dropping it over the side. "Wait! Don't we need that to escape?" asked Peter as he watched the robot leg fall.

"Naw, we only needed the armband and the battery. I was just kidding about the leg," shrugged Rocket.

"What?" Peter shouted.

"I thought it'd be funny! Was it funny? Was he hopping all around?"

"I had to transfer fifteen thousand credits to him," Peter complained.

"Silence! Let's hurry and escape this wretched hole," said Drax as he pulled himself over the railing to stand next to Peter.

Gamora was shocked to see Drax joining in on the escape plan. "What is he doing here?" Gamora asked Peter angrily.

"If I told you the answer was 'being a total nut job,' would that surprise you?" responded Peter.

"No, I mean, why are you allowing him to come with us?" Gamora demanded.

Peter looked embarrassed. "He sorta saved my life."

"And we could use him," added Rocket as he jerked open the tower door and rushed inside.

"I am Groot," Groot contributed as he followed Rocket inside.

"This is a mistake," Gamora said, narrowing her eyes at Drax.

Drax stared back at her, but he said nothing.

Inside the tower, Rocket wired the quarnyx battery into a bank of controls.

Peter looked out the window, checking out the action in the yard.

"Uh...I don't mean to worry you, Rocket, but those are some pretty big weapons," he said, pointing down to two arriving Nova Guards with giant shoulder-mounted rocket launchers. The guards aimed the launchers up at the tower where they were standing.

"I'm working, I'm working," assured Rocket as he stripped two wires and tied them together.

"Oh, I remember your kind of animal," Drax suddenly said. "We used to roast them over a flaming pit as children! They were delicious."

"Not helping!" Rocket shouted at Drax.

KA-BOOOOM! The whole watchtower shook as one of the Novas' rockets slammed into the neck of the tower below their floor!

"Almost got it, almost got it..." Rocket said as the tower still shook.

"They're about to fire again!" said Peter, watching the guards out the window.

"Got it!" shouted Rocket.

Peter watched as the guards, the prisoners, and the whole station suddenly floated off the ground!

"He's turned off the gravity everywhere but inside this tower," Gamora excitedly observed.

"Hold on," Rocket warned as he threw another switch. The watchtower, which had been built in pieces, released its grip on the top floor, where Rocket and the others were standing.

Now free from the rest of the tower, the top floor started to float away.

"Great, we're in the floating top floor of a tower. This helps us how?" asked Peter.

"Watch and learn, humie," said Rocket, working on another set of controls. Suddenly the hover-bots that had been swarming Groot before now flew toward the floating floor and gripped onto it.

Using one of the controls like a joystick, Rocket guided the hover-bots as they pushed the tower floor in whatever direction he chose.

"Told you it was a good plan." Rocket smiled as he flew their floor out of the yard like a big, square spaceship. Peter and the others left the chaos of the riot far behind them.

Rocket guided the floor to a section of the station where the prisoners' belongings were stored. Everyone went straight for the storage unit that held Peter's belongings.

"It's here," Peter shouted as he found the Orb in his backpack. "The Orb is here!" Everyone let out a sigh of relief. But Peter kept searching in the pack, searching for his headphones, the ones from Earth that he'd seen the guard with earlier. Awesome Mix Tape #1 wasn't there!

Peter handed his backpack to Gamora. "Take this and go to my ship, called the *Milano*. It's the orange-and-blue one in the corner of the impound yard."

Peter turned to run back toward the station. "Wait, where are you going?" Gamora asked.

"Something of mine is still in there," said Peter.

"How do you expect to—?"

"Just go. I'll meet you at the *Milano*."

And with that, Peter ran back toward the chaos of the riot.

Gamora, looking confused, led the others toward the *Milano*.

# CHAPTER 6

*A* team of Nova Corps guards waited impatiently as the huge metal vault-like door to the impound area slowly opened. They'd been ordered to detain the prisoners who'd shut off the gravity and flown away with the top floor of the security tower, and the Corps guards knew if they came back without capturing those prisoners, their jobs were on the line. They fidgeted nervously as the door finally opened.

It had never even occurred to them that one of the escapees might come back. That's why the sight of Peter Quill coming toward them through the now-open impound doorway was such a surprise!

And that surprise was all Peter needed. A pistol in each hand, he stunned the entire team of guards before they managed to raise their weapons.

"Where are my tunes?" Peter shouted, as he ran past the fallen guards.

Gamora led Rocket, Groot, and Drax aboard the *Milano*. Once in the cockpit, Rocket started booting up the ship's controls.

"How's he supposed to get to us?" Rocket asked Gamora, annoyed.

"He declined to share that info with me," Gamora stated.

"Well, forget this!" shouted Rocket. "I'm not waiting around for some rotten humie with a death wish. Let's get out of here. You have the Orb, right?"

"Yes, it's right here," said Gamora, opening Peter's backpack. But when she looked in, there was no Orb after all. "Oh! That lying, thieving rat!"

**D**eep inside the station, Peter casually tossed the Orb in the air as he neared the main office. Inside, the guard who had stolen his headphones was still sitting at his desk, bopping his head to Peter's favorite songs. This guy didn't even seem to know there was a riot going on! He was apparently missing the whole thing while grooving to Awesome Mix Tape #1.

Peter lifted the Orb in the air and tapped the guard on the shoulder to get his attention. When the guard looked up, Peter slammed the Orb against his head.

"Told you those were mine," Peter said to the dazed guard as he pulled the headphones off him.

Now Peter had to get back to his ship. The hallway he'd just passed through would be teeming with guards by now. But as he looked out the office window into space, another path to the ship occurred to him.

Back on the *Milano*, tensions were running high.

"I'm not waiting here to be blown to bits," shouted Rocket, jumping into the pilot seat.

Rocket guided the ship out of the space dock doors, when, suddenly, he saw something he never expected to see—Peter Quill flying through space! Wearing his protective mask, which was not meant for the dangers of deep space, he was using the rocket boosters on his boots to do an unscheduled space walk!

"It's official," Rocket said. "This guy is crazy!"

As the others watched in disbelief as Peter flew toward them, Drax started to smile.

Entering the ship's interior through a decompression tube, Peter pulled the mask off his face and gulped the air of the ship. He was dizzy and red-faced, but Drax slapped him on the back proudly.

"Rocketing through space without the proper gear! Ha!" observed Drax, pleased. "This one shows spirit! He will be a keen ally in the battle against Ronan. Companion, what were you retrieving?"

Peter pulled the headphones out of his jacket and showed them to Drax.

Drax looked at them blankly. "Some kind of a...a music player?"

Peter nodded. Drax's whole expression changed.

"You are an imbecile," he said darkly.

"That he is," confirmed Gamora.

"Maybe," admitted Peter. "But I also have this," he said, pulling the Orb from his jacket.

"Ha! The payday!" shouted Rocket with excitement. He and Groot looked at each other with a smug sense of satisfaction.

"You will sell this object?" asked Drax. "I should be a part of this plan."

Peter groaned. Someone else who wanted a piece of the pie. "What would you spend the money on, a shirt?"

"What need do I have of a shirt?" asked Drax, confused.

"Uh-huh," nodded Peter. "That's what I thought you'd say."

Shaking his head, Drax continued. "Any money I make will go to finance my war on Ronan. What is the object's price?"

Rocket, Peter, and Gamora all looked at one another.

"Eighty thousand units," Peter said.

"Four billion units," Gamora said at the same time.

Rocket squealed in frustration at Gamora. "What did you tell him the real price for? You ruined it!"

Gamora shrugged. "I was raised to hurt heathens, not to lie."

"Now that I have joined you, I will take an equal share," said Drax.

"Fine, we split it four ways," agreed Peter. But a loud moan from Groot made him quickly backtrack. "Sorry, I mean five ways!"

Peter picked the Orb up and looked at it before continuing. "That said, I think it's fair we know what's in it."

"I don't know," admitted Gamora.

"Considering who's after it, it must be some kind of weapon," Peter said, thinking out loud.

"I'm selling it to a collector who wants it for archival purposes only," said Gamora. "Whatever it is, he'll keep it secure."

Drax took the Orb from Peter's hands. "If it's a weapon, why don't we see if we can use it to destroy Ronan?" Running his hands over the seam of the Orb, Drax started trying to pry it open...until Gamora unsheathed her sword.

"Put it down, you fool," she said, showing him the glint off her blade. "You could hurt us all!"

Angry, Drax lifted the Orb above his head as if he might smash Gamora with it. "Or I could just destroy you!"

Peter quickly jumped between them. "Okay, everybody! Just chill out here! We're supposed to be partners!"

Gamora snatched the Orb out of Drax's hands. "We have an agreement. We're not partners. I have never relied on anyone. I will not begin now. I will tell my connection that we're on the way to bring him the Orb."

Gamora spun on her heels and marched out of the room. After she was out of earshot, Peter said, "Man, I'm getting to really like her."

Rocket looked at Peter and shook his head in disgust. "You've got issues, Quill," he said as he also walked away.

Drax looked uneasily at Peter, and then followed Rocket out, saying, "I'll be in my bunk."

"That's my bunk, actually," said Peter. "My ship, my bedroom, but..."

It was too late. Drax was gone. Peter realized he was alone with Groot on the bridge. "Just you and me, huh?" the human asked the tree alien.

Groot held his hand up and out to Peter.

"You...you want me to give you a high-five?" asked Peter.

Peter tried to meet the alien's palm, but Groot quickly grabbed his face and shook it around a bit, bellowing a laugh that sounded like a seal.

"Hey! What?!" protested Peter. "Stop it, man!"

Groot let him go but chuckled a little more under his breath as he lumbered away.

"That's not cool!" Peter shouted after the

departing Groot. "It didn't even make sense. You have a weird sense of humor!"

Now alone on the bridge of his ship, Peter slumped into the pilot's chair. "Yeah, this is a great group I've stumbled into," he muttered to himself. "Just great."

# CHAPTER 7

**S**oon after the *Milano*'s escape, Ronan's ship, the *Dark Aster*, attacked Kyln station. Already damaged from the riot and short on staff, the station didn't have adequate defenses to fight against Ronan's assault. His forces tore through the walls like they were made out of paper and had both the inmates and the guards under control before a distress call could even be sent out.

As Ronan strode through the station, he was

flooded with memories. When he was younger, the Nova Corps had arrested him for carrying out a justified retribution on a small planet—a planet so weak that it didn't deserve to exist. The Nova Corps had sent him here, to Kyln. He had been held in this very station, slept in one of these very cells.

It was here that he had met the Exolon monks who taught him that "strength" is the only truth... and that it is a sin not to use it. It was here that Ronan discovered his dark destiny—to crush the universe under his might.

As Ronan reminisced, Nebula approached him. "The Nova Corps have sent a fleet to defend the prison. It should be here shortly."

"And Gamora?" asked Ronan.

"Gone," Nebula replied reluctantly, bowing her head.

"Send the Necrocraft to every corner of the

quadrant," commanded Ronan, his anger rising. "Find the Orb. At any price. By any means."

Nebula bowed again, acknowledging Ronan's will. "And...this place?" she asked.

"The Nova Corps can't learn what we're searching for," said Ronan. "Cleanse it. Leave nothing behind."

**O**n the deck of the *Milano*, Peter asked Gamora, "What destination should I chart for us in the ship's computer?"

"Knowhere," Gamora replied.

"Nowhere?" Wasn't the plan to go find this big buyer of hers, the one who would pay so much for the Orb?

"No, not 'nowhere'," signed an exasperated Gamora. "Knowhere."

Half a day later, in the depths of space, in the middle of nowhere, they finally arrived at Knowhere.

It was a space colony like no other Peter had ever seen—the size of a large meteor, but in the shape of a giant skull.

"Uh...what is this?" he asked Gamora.

"It's the severed head of an ancient celestial being," Gamora reported matter-of-factly, as if this were the most normal information in the galaxy.

"I hope whatever cut it off isn't still around," quipped Peter as he steered the ship through one of the giant skull's eye sockets, which was used as the space dock. "Heads up. We're going in!" he called.

Flying inside, Peter saw colorful shacks built into the bone walls. Miners flying single-person space pods were drilling into spots around the skull, extracting what looked like a yellow viscous fluid.

"Hundred of years ago, workers were sent in to mine the organic matter left in the skull," explained Gamora. "Brain tissue, spinal fluid. It's dangerous, illegal work suitable only for outlaws."

"Then I should be at home here," claimed Peter. "I'm from a planet of outlaws. Billy the Kid, Bonnie and Clyde..."

"Sounds like a place I'd like to visit," said Drax, joining them on deck.

"Cool," replied Peter.

"Visit, and then *battle*!" continued Drax, excited at the idea of combat.

Peter rolled his eyes as he pulled into a parking area.

**O**nce Peter stopped the *Milano* and paid an outrageously high docking fee, everyone unloaded from the ship. They walked through the streets of what would have been a typical small mining town, if it weren't for the surreal fact that it was built inside a giant dead alien's head.

Getting to Gamora's buyer was taking longer than they expected, since whenever the group came across children, Groot would stop and sprout flowers for them. This delighted the kids but annoyed his fellow travelers, who would just as soon get the sale over with so they could get out of here, split their earnings, and never see each other again.

"So, where is this buyer of yours?" Rocket asked Gamora.

But before she could answer, Peter saw

something that alarmed him. He quickly shoved the others into an alleyway and peeked out.

Yondu and a few of the other Ravagers were across the street.

"Spread out," the leader told his men. "Find Quill. Remember, he might be calling himself Star-Lord." The others did as they were told and scattered themselves among the crowd.

Yondu had recently visited the Broker on Xandar. It hadn't taken much threatening for Yondu to discover the location of the person looking to buy the Orb. Peter would have to come here if he wanted to sell that thing, which meant that all Yondu had to do was sit and wait. Sooner or later that ungrateful traitor would come to him.

"Where did the Broker say this buyer was located?" Yondu asked his second in command.

"The Broker said the place was kind of hidden," the other Ravager explained.

Peter ducked as Yondu and his companion walked right by the mouth of the alley where he was hiding. After Yondu passed, Peter stuck his head back out and looked. They were gone—for now. Relieved, he looked back at his companions, only to see them staring at him.

"Friend of yours?" asked Gamora.

"Not exactly," admitted Peter.

On the lookout for more Ravagers, the team followed Gamora to a run-down miner's club called the Boot of Jemiah. The place seemed a lot like the people inside: loud, ugly, and smelly.

"Your buyer's in here?" asked Peter, surprised that someone with enough cash to pay for the Orb would hang out in such a low-rent establishment.

"No, my buyer owns this place," Gamora explained as they stepped inside.

Drax looked around. "What shall we do while we wait?" he asked.

"Oh," said Rocket, a smile crossing his face, "I bet we can think of something."

Within minutes, Rocket had shown Groot and Drax the small track where Orloni races were held. The Orloni, small, ratlike rodents, raced down a track to escape a hungry frog-beast called a F'Saki. Rocket loved Orloni races, and the competition naturally appealed to Drax.

Meanwhile, on the other side of the room, Gamora and Peter sat at a table.

"My connection is really making us wait," Gamora complained.

"That's a negotiation thing," explained Peter. "Nobody wants to seem desperate. I've done lots of deals. Your thing is more just: 'Stab, stab, stab...Those are my terms!'"

"My 'father' didn't stress diplomacy," Gamora explained simply.

"By 'father,' you mean Thanos?" asked Peter.

Gamora nodded. "Once, after he had kidnapped me, I asked, 'Why?'...But there was no 'why.' The strong devour the weak. That's how he sees the universe."

Peter got a look in his eye like he understood. "That guy we were hiding from before? Yondu? Similar vibe. When he took me from Earth, he drilled it in my head: Nice guys finish dead."

Gamora looked at Peter almost like she was seeing him for the first time. "So we both turned against the men who raised us."

Peter shook his head kind of sadly. "No," he said. "I didn't turn against Yondu...I turned *into* him." He stopped for a moment, contemplating this, then continued by asking, "How come you flipped?"

"My family taught me to believe in strength, and I do," said Gamora. "But we just have different ideas of what strength is."

Peter nodded, understanding. Were they actually bonding here?

"And what's this?" Gamora asked, pointing to the headphones sticking out of Peter's pocket. Peter pulled them out.

"My mother's music," he explained. "She loved to share her music with me. I just happened to have it on me when she...I mean, when I left Earth."

Peter slipped the headphones over Gamora's ears and hit play. She cocked her head, listening to a slow jam.

"What...what do you do with it?" Gamora asked.

"Do? With music?" replied Peter. "Nothing. You listen to it. You dance."

"I am a warrior and an assassin," stated Gamora flatly, talking a little too loudly with the headphones going in her ears. "I do not dance."

"You can dance," assured Peter. "I've seen you fight. Dancing is all about rhythm and flow. You just have to leave out the hurting people."

Peter stood up, pulling her with him. He took her arms and showed her how to move. "Like this," he said. They started dancing. Gamora was clearly amazed at what she was allowing herself to do.

"What's the point of this?" she asked, but she didn't stop moving.

"There isn't one," Peter admitted.

At that moment there was a sudden crash from across the club. Peter and Gamora turned to see Rocket, Groot, and Drax in the middle of a fight at the Orloni table.

They broke off from their dance and ran to help.

# CHAPTER 8

Peter and Gamora sprinted for the Orloni table and pulled the fighting Drax and Rocket apart. "Whoa! Whoa! Whoa! What're you doing?" asked Peter.

"This vermin laid hands on me!" shouted Drax, as Gamora held him back.

"That is true!" confirmed Rocket.

"He has no respect!" Drax shouted even louder.

"That is also true! He keeps calling me 'vermin,'"

Rocket complained. "He thinks I'm some stupid thing! Well, I didn't ask to get made!"

Peter tried to calm him down. "No one thinks you're a—"

But Rocket pushed Peter off. "He called me 'vermin'! She called me 'rodent'!"

Gamora was taken aback. "Rocket, my intent was not malicious."

But Rocket ignored her and threatened Drax.

"Let's see if you can still laugh after I finish with you!"

Peter jumped between the two of them. "Four billion units, Rocket! Suck it up for one more lousy night and you're rich!"

That got Rocket's attention. He took a deep breath and looked around at all of them. "Fine...."

While Rocket had calmed down somewhat, Drax was still enraged. He broke free of Gamora and headed for the exit. "We have traveled halfway across the quadrant and all I have done is quarrel with wildlife," complained Drax as he left. "Ronan is no closer to paying for his crimes!"

And with that, Drax walked outside, leaving Peter to call after him.

"Let him go. We don't need him," said Gamora to Peter.

"We? You got a mouse in your pocket?" said Peter, growing sick of this partnership. "You guys better find a ride home, because the minute we get what we came for, I don't want to see any of you maniacs again."

Groot, who had been lurking nearby during all the shouting, stepped forward and asked, "I am Groot?"

"Yes," confirmed Peter, "you're also a maniac!" But then he realized what had just happened. "I think I just spoke Groot. It's disturbing."

At that moment, a hidden panel in one of the

club's walls opened up, and a small female stepped forward, addressing Gamora. "Milady, I am Carina. I am here to fetch you for my master."

Gamora, Peter, Groot, and Rocket looked at one another. Finally, it was go time. They followed Carina through a secret passage into a dark tunnel. After some distance, the tunnel opened up into a large room lined with glass cages. The cages were filled with animals, plants, and other life forms that were less easily classified.

Peter gave off a low whistle as he looked through a window into a hallway. This combination zoo-museum went on for as far as his eye could see. It seemed to stretch on forever.

Carina led the group onward to an examination bay while explaining, "We house the galaxy's largest collection of fauna, relics, and species of all manner."

An odd-looking white-haired man entered from

the back of the lab. Carina introduced him: "I present to you Taneleer Tivan. He is known as the Collector."

The Collector stepped forward, "Ah! My dear Gamora. Finally we meet... in the flesh."

"Let's bypass the formalities, Tivan," Gamora spat out impatiently. "We have the item we discussed." She pulled out the Orb and showed it to him.

The Collector glanced at the Orb and then looked away, seeing Groot. "Oh that... My, what do we have here?"

"I am Groot," Groot explained, a little miffed by the question.

"A Groot! Fascinating," exclaimed the Collector, excited. "You must allow me to pay you a small fee now so that I may own your carcass at the moment of your death."

Groot shrugged.

The Collector smiled, pleased, and then moved his attention to Rocket. "And what is this little beast? Is this its pet?"

"It's *what*?!?" shouted Rocket.

Seeing where this was likely to go, Gamora interrupted. "Tivan, we've been halfway around the galaxy retrieving this Orb."

"Well then, let us see what you've brought," said the Collector, taking the Orb and placing it onto an examination table. After a moment spent carefully looking it over, the Collector smiled. "Yes...this is authentic," pronounced the Collector.

"An authentic what?" asked Peter.

"An ancient source of great power," said the Collector casually. "Does it matter?"

"Not as long as you pay what you promised," said Gamora, cutting Peter off.

"Of course," said the Collector, using a special

device to open the Orb slightly so that he, and only he, could peer inside. "I have not become the universe's foremost collector of rare items by reneging on my—"

Suddenly Carina rushed forward and reached for the Orb. "I will be your servant no more!" she shouted. She had been watching and waiting for a moment such as this. For years she'd suffered under the cruel hand of the Collector, who badly mistreated her and her fellow servants. She had heard the Collector talking about this Orb and the power that it held, and she was convinced that if she could hold such power in her hand, she would be able to free herself from her cruel master.

But, unfortunately for Carina, she didn't understand the nature of that power.

"Carina, no!" shouted the Collector...but it was too late.

The second Carina touched the Orb, her whole

body convulsed! Her eyes bulged and turned black, her face distorted with energy. A harsh white glow came out from inside of her body.

Almost instinctively, Groot grabbed Rocket and ran back down the tunnel, away from whatever was going to happen. At the same moment, Gamora grabbed Peter, dragging him down to the ground for cover. Barely a heartbeat later, there was a pulse of bright white light!

The sheer force of the explosion blasted all of the glass cages, every item the Collector had assembled.

The Collector wailed as he saw this. "My life's work!" he screamed moments before a flying piece of scrap metal hit him and knocked him out.

Gamora and Peter, now that the explosion was over, pulled themselves back up. They looked around, seeing everything destroyed.

"I was a fool!" shouted Gamora. "How could I think Tivan could contain whatever was within the Orb? I was blinded by my own selfish desires." She grabbed the Orb, and the pair made their way through the tunnel to join Groot and Rocket back in the club.

As soon as they walked out of the secret passage, Rocket spied the Orb in her hand and started freaking out. "What do you still have it for?" he asked incredulously.

"What are we going to do?" Peter responded. "Leave it there?"

"We must bring this to the Nova Corps. There's a chance they can contain it," Gamora explained.

Rocket's eyes went wide. "Are you kidding me? We're wanted by the Nova Corps. Just give it to Ronan!"

"We cannot allow the Orb to fall into Ronan's

hands," said Gamora. "After all he's done, after all I helped him to do! We must go back to your ship and deliver it to Nova officers!" Gamora walked out of the club.

"Or we bring it to someone who's not going to arrest us," Peter suggested as he and Rocket followed Gamora. "Someone with a whole lot of money."

The second the trio walked out into the street, they saw Drax, his back to them and his arms outstretched with a blade in each hand. He laughed like a maniac and looked up at several Necrocraft from the fleet of Ronan.

"At last, I shall meet my foe and destroy him!" said Drax, watching the ships come in for a landing.

"Oh no," said Peter. "Ronan knows we're here!"

Once again, it was time to run.

# CHAPTER 9

**"S**tand behind me!" Drax shouted to his companions, a smile on his face. "You may write of this tale in your storybooks, so that future generations shall delight in its telling!"

"I am Groot?" asked Groot.

"Yes, he is insane," said Rocket, answering Groot's question.

"Sanity is the refuge of cowards!" Drax declared.

Peter figured this was about the worst situation he'd ever been in and was about to say that it simply couldn't get worse. Then it did.

"Quill!" shouted a voice from across the street. Peter looked up to see Yondu. He and the other Ravagers were running right for Peter!

Gamora moved quickly. Grabbing Peter, she ran off with Rocket and Groot on her tail. The Ravagers, seeing the Orb still in Gamora's hand, gave chase. They ran past Drax, who held his ground in the street, watching, pleased, as all the Necrocraft now opened their doors.

Gamora ran up a ramp onto a loading station where a miner was anchoring his pod to a dock. Gamora grabbed the miner. "Try to curl up as you land," she advised him. He looked confused until she physically threw him off the ramp and down to the street below.

The mining pods were the kind Peter had seen from the *Milano* when they'd first docked at Knowhere. Small, single-person capsules with jets, they had robotic arms mounted to the front that were primarily used for operating mining equipment that drilled into the bone walls of the station.

Gamora quickly loaded herself into one pod, Peter into another, and Rocket into a third. "Sorry," shouted Rocket to Groot as his pod took off. "Not enough room for two. We'll be back for you, big guy." Groot watched sadly as his friends zipped away.

By the time Yondu and the Ravagers reached the pod ramp, everyone was gone but Groot.

"**R**onan the Accuser!" Drax shouted as he saw his sworn enemy exit one of the Necrocraft. The day of vengeance Drax had dreamed of was finally here! The battle, he was sure, would be glorious.

Ronan strode right up to Drax. "Who are you? Where is Gamora?"

"You destroyed my planet…my people," shouted Drax, ignoring the question. "I challenge you to combat under Arisheim's Law."

"You're joking," sneered Ronan. "Those antiquated decrees mean nothing to me. I don't even know who you are."

Drax proudly proclaimed, "I am Drax…the Destroyer!"

But the conversation was interrupted when Nebula ran up to Ronan and shouted, "Gamora is escaping with the Orb!"

Without another thought for Drax, Ronan

turned and followed Nebula as she ran back to her Necrocraft. Drax's worst nightmare was unfolding. He had faced Ronan and had been ignored!

Several of Ronan's Sakaaran soldiers flew their Necrocraft in pursuit of the much slower mining pods that Gamora, Rocket, and Peter were trying to escape in. But it quickly became clear that their main focus was Gamora. Since she was drawing their fire, Peter knew it was up to him and Rocket to try to deal with the ships.

"These pods are industrial grade," Peter shouted to Rocket over the pod's communicator. "They're nearly indestructible."

"Not against Necro-blasts they're not!" warned Rocket.

"That's not what I mean," said Peter.

"Oh..." said Rocket. Seeing Peter's meaning, Rocket turned his pod on a dime and smashed it right into one of the Necrocraft pursuing Gamora. The ship smoked and fell away as Rocket's pod burst out through the roof. Rocket immediately turned his pod toward a second Necrocraft, bashing into it as well.

"That little guy sure can fly!" said Peter as he admired Rocket's skills with the pod. Then he flew his own pod over the top of another of the Necrocraft. Inside, the Sakaaran pilot heard a ripping sound and looked up.

"Yo! How about I borrow your ride?" Peter said to the pilot as he used the arms on the front of his pod to pry the roof off the alien ship. The Sakaaran pilot was instantly blown into space.

Peter then dropped his pod down inside the

ship. Peter used the pod's arms to control the Necrocraft! He used the guns to blast at other Necrocraft! They were doing it! They were really striking back at Ronan's fleet!

But that's when Peter got a transmission from Gamora.

"Quill! I'm trapped! I have to go up!" she screamed. Cornered by too many Necrocraft, she flew her pod through a hole in Knowhere and out into deep space!

Back on the ground, Drax wasn't about to let Ronan get away. With the villain's back turned, Drax raised his sword and ran at him. But just before impact, Ronan spun, grabbed Drax's sword, and cast it aside. Then he grabbed Drax by the throat and hurled him into a nearby food cart! Drax was down and Ronan had barely broken stride, as if he'd swatted at an insect.

Chasing after the Necrocraft, Peter and Rocket flew their pods out of the same chasm in the giant skull, but when they got outside, they saw Gamora's ship pointed straight at a nearby black hole.

"I'll never make it to the *Milano*," Gamora transmitted to Peter. "I have no choice. I'm going into the black hole. It's the only hope we have of destroying the Orb!"

"What...? Wait!" shouted the incredulous Peter.

Pulling himself up, Drax made another run at Ronan, but this time Ronan slammed him to the ground.

Ronan laughed in amusement at Drax's pathetic attempts to escape his grasp. "I have destroyed so many planets that I don't remember destroying yours," sneered Ronan. "And I doubt I will remember destroying you."

With that he hurled Drax into one of the nearby yellow pools of waste chemicals by the side of the road.

Nebula's Necrocraft now arrived behind Gamora's pod.

"You're a disappointment, sister!" shouted Nebula over the communicator. "When you took the

Orb, I thought you were massing a force, not hiding amongst rabble."

"Nebula," Gamora tried. "If Ronan and Thanos get this Orb, no one in the universe will be safe. They'll get us all!"

"Not *all*, sister," sneered Nebula. "You'll already be dead."

With a shot she blasted the pod to pieces, sending Gamora's body out into the void of space, and leaving the Orb up for grabs.

As Ronan walked away from Drax, he got a call from Nebula on his communicator. "Brother, it is done," said Nebula. "I'm bringing the Orb to you now." Ronan smiled.

Peter, from inside his pod, stared helplessly at Gamora's floating body. She wouldn't be able to last out there for long!

"Quill! Come on, we have to go," urged Rocket from his pod. "These mining pods aren't meant to be out here. There's hardly any atmosphere. There's nothing we can do for her."

Peter knew that Rocket's words were true. "Yeah, I'm coming," he said.

But Peter couldn't bear to pilot to his pod away from her body. Instead, he tried something else.

"Yondu, are you there? This is Quill!" said Peter, tuning his communicator to a frequency often used by the Ravagers. "I'm at coordinates 227-k32-8524, right outside Knowhere," continued Peter. "If you're here, come and get me. I'm all yours!"

"Quill! What are you doing?" shouted Rocket to

Peter over the radio. "Whatever you do, don't—"
But, cutting the radio, Peter didn't hear the end
of Rocket's sentence. He was too busy doing the
exact thing that Rocket was telling him not to do.

He nervously put on his helmet and hooked
himself up to life support. He popped open the
door to his mining pod, letting the air inside rush
out into the void of space. Then he leaped from
the pod, shooting off his boot rockets, and headed
straight for Gamora.

Gamora's alien race was tough, their bodies
strong. But even Gamora couldn't withstand the
vacuum of space for very long. When Peter reached
her, he could see that her skin was starting to
crack. There was no question...she was almost
gone.

"No," Peter shouted inside of his mask. "Hold
on!" But the sound of his encouragement could
never reach Gamora's ears, surrounded as they

were by the absence of matter. In a desperate move, Peter reached behind his head where the air tube flowed into his mask and pulled it out. He yanked the tube around and put it into Gamora's mouth, trying to buy her a few extra precious breaths of oxygen.

Seeing all this, Rocket was horrified. "Quill, no! Quill! You're going to die! You'll die in seconds! Quill! Quill!!!" But all he could do was watch Peter's actions unfold...watch Peter throw his life away for a lost cause!

Peter could already feel himself going numb. He looked into Gamora's face. There were so many things that Peter had wanted to do in this universe and so many things he had wanted to see. He regretted those undone things, but he was a little surprised to realize that he didn't regret trying to save Gamora. Somehow, putting someone else first, even if it meant dying, felt good to him in a way that he never expected it would. After thinking this, he let out his last breath....

And then, Peter's whole world exploded into a bright white light.

# CHAPTER 10

As Peter and Gamora were bathed in white light, he thought, "I'm supposed to walk into the light, aren't I?" But he couldn't walk; he couldn't even move. He lost consciousness.

When he woke up, he was still next to Gamora, but now on the floor of Yondu's craft. The white light had been its headlights as it approached to get them. They were saved! His last-minute gamble on Yondu's need for revenge had worked!

Gamora coughed to wakefulness next to him. "How...how are we here?" she asked.

"I've gone and done something incredibly noble." Peter smiled, pleased with himself.

Back on the surface of Knowhere, Drax's limp body sank to the bottom of the fetid yellow pool—until suddenly two leafy tendrils reached down and wrapped themselves around him. Groot pulled Drax to the surface, sliding his body onto dry land.

Drax sputtered awake! Stepping in front of Groot, Rocket leaned down to examine Drax.

"Blasted idiot!" Rocket shouted at Drax as he came to. "I'm surrounded by idiots! Quill just got himself captured! And none of this would have happened if you didn't try to single-handedly take on a whole army!"

Still recovering, Drax nodded at this. "You're

right. I was a fool. All my puffery was just to distract me from the emotions of my loss."

"Oh, boo-hoo. *I'm Drax and my planet is dead....*" ranted Rocket.

Groot covered his mouth in shock at Rocket's insensitive comments. Rocket looked at him. "I don't care if it's mean. Everybody's lost something. Everybody's seen tragedy. That's no reason to get the rest of us hurt!"

Drax thought about this as Rocket stood up straight and turned to walk away. "Come on, Groot. Ronan has the Orb now. The only chance we have is to get to the other side of the universe as fast as we can, and maybe, just maybe, we'll be able to live full lives before that whack job ever gets there."

But Groot didn't follow Rocket. He just called after him, "I am Groot!"

"I know Peter and Gamora are the only friends we've ever had," responded Rocket. "But there's an army of Ravagers around them and only two of us!"

"Three," said Drax. "There's three of us."

On board the Ravager ship, Peter took another brutal hit to his stomach. "Oof," he groaned.

"Stop it!" shouted Gamora. Several strong Ravagers held her back. "Leave him alone!"

"After all I've done for you, this is how you repay me?" Yondu said.

"When I picked you up, these boys wanted to eat you! They'd never eaten a human being before. I stopped them. I saved your life!"

Peter straightened up and looked Yondu in the eyes. "Oh, will you shut up? You've been throwing that in my face for twenty years. Like that's some big thing, not eating me! Normal people don't even think about eating someone else, much less expect that person to be thankful for it!"

Yondu thought about this for a moment, and then responded by punching Peter again. "Ouch! Look, Yondu, Ronan has the Orb. It's so powerful that—"

"I know what he's got," said Yondu. "I've been to see the Broker."

"Then you know that if he uses it, it'll wipe out the Nova Corps. Billions all over the galaxy will die."

"Who cares? Not my business," said Yondu, before turning to the other Ravagers in the room. "Let's teach Quill what happens when you betray us!"

As the Ravagers closed in, Peter shouted,

"Hurt me and you'll miss the biggest score of your life."

That comment stopped all of the outlaws in their tracks.

"What score?" asked Yondu.

"The Orb, of course," explained Peter.

"No way..." Yondu said. "It's with Ronan on the *Dark Aster*, the most defended ship in the galaxy. How would you—?"

"I've got an inside man," said Peter, pointing to Gamora.

Gamora took her cue. "I lived on the *Dark Aster* for seven years. It does have weaknesses—and I am one of the few people in the universe who knows what they are."

Yondu considered this. There would be a certain satisfaction in hurting Peter Quill, it was true...but stealing from Ronan, right out from under his very nose, and becoming rich in the process? Yondu decided that kind of satisfaction would be even better.

"You've got a deal," Yondu said, shaking hands with Peter, then throwing his arm around him as if he hadn't been, less than a minute ago, beating him silly. "How do we get started?"

But before Peter could answer, a communication screen burst to life. "Attention, idiots!" said Rocket on the screen. "The lunatic on top of this ship has a Hadron Enforcer, a weapon of my own design. If you don't hand over our companions now, he's going to tear your ship apart!"

Everyone on the Ravager ship ran to the window to see that, sure enough, Rocket was flying the *Milano*, and Drax was sitting on top of it wearing a space suit and pointing a massive weapon at them.

"I'll give you until the count of five," said Rocket.

"Five?" asked Gamora in alarm.

Rocket immediately started counting down. "Five...four..."

Peter ran to the communicator screen. "No, wait!" he screamed. "Rocket, it's me! We're fine. We've worked it out!"

Rocket's whole demeanor changed. "Oh, hey! What's up, Quill!"

"What were you doing?" asked Peter.

"Saving you, of course," said Rocket. "That's what friends do."

"I am Groot," Peter heard Groot say from just offscreen.

"Fine! Yes, it was Groot's idea...." admitted Rocket, sullen.

"But five seconds?" asked Peter. "How would they have turned us over that quickly? You would have blasted us, too!"

"Look," said Rocket, "you can pick apart the plan if you want, but it worked, didn't it?"

"No, we were already...Oh, fine....Yes, it worked," sighed Peter. "Just get over here. We've got some planning to do."

# EPILOGUE

Years later, they would all look back to that moment on the Ravager ship as one of the most important days of their lives. It was the day that a kidnapped child of Earth, a warrior daughter of Thanos, a broken man bent on revenge, a mutated fur-covered genius, and a living tree first banded together to defend the galaxy.

Rogues, criminals, slackers, outlaws, escaped

convicts...they were all of these things. But when the greatest threats the galaxy had ever faced, Ronan and Thanos, got their hands on a power source capable of destroying the universe, these five defenders answered the call.

None of them expected to become heroes. Nor did they expect to even be friends. But when the circumstances forced them to, they rose to the occasion. They became—guardians.

They had first joined forces with the goal of getting rich, which they never did. But over years of journeys together, they found much, *much* more. Rocket and Groot found companionship and belonging. Drax found a way to honor his lost planet. Gamora discovered how to escape the poisonous family that raised her. And Peter went on to connect with the tenderness he had lost as a child after his mother's death.

They also learned the unbelievable secret of that mysterious energy source that resonated within the Orb.

But that—that's another story....